D0908420

ERIC CARLE
Rooster Is Off
to See the World

by Eric Carle

READY-TO-READ

SIMON SPOTLIGHT
New York   London   Toronto   Sydney   New Delhi
This book was previously published with slightly different text as *Rooster's Off to See the World*.

SIMON SPOTLIGHT

An imprint of Simon & Schuster Children's Publishing Division

1230 Avenue of the Americas, New York, New York 10020

Copyright © 1972 by Eric Carle Corp.

Eric Carle's name and signature logo type are registered trademarks of Eric Carle.

First Simon Spotlight Ready-to-Read edition 2013

Manufactured in China 1215 SCP

10 9 8 7 6 5 4 3 2 1

ISBN 978-1-4814-7182-4

This book was previously published with slightly different text as *Rooster's Off to See the World*.

One morning a rooster set
out to see the world.
He had not gone far
when he began to feel lonely.

Then the rooster met two cats.

"Come with me to see

the world," said the rooster.

"We would love to,"

said the cats.

So they set off

down the road.

Then the rooster and the
cats met three frogs.
"Would you like to see the
world?" asked the rooster.

"Why not?" said the frogs.

"We are not busy now."

So the frogs followed

the rooster and the cats.

Then the rooster, the cats,

and the frogs met

four turtles.

"Would you like to see the

world?" asked the rooster.

"It might be fun,"

snapped one of the turtles.

So they all set off

to see the world.

Then the rooster, the cats,
the frogs, and the turtles
saw five fish.

The fish asked
where they were going.

"We're off to see the world,"

said the rooster.

The fish wanted to join them,

so they all set off

to see the world.

Soon it got dark.

"Where is our dinner?"

asked the cats.

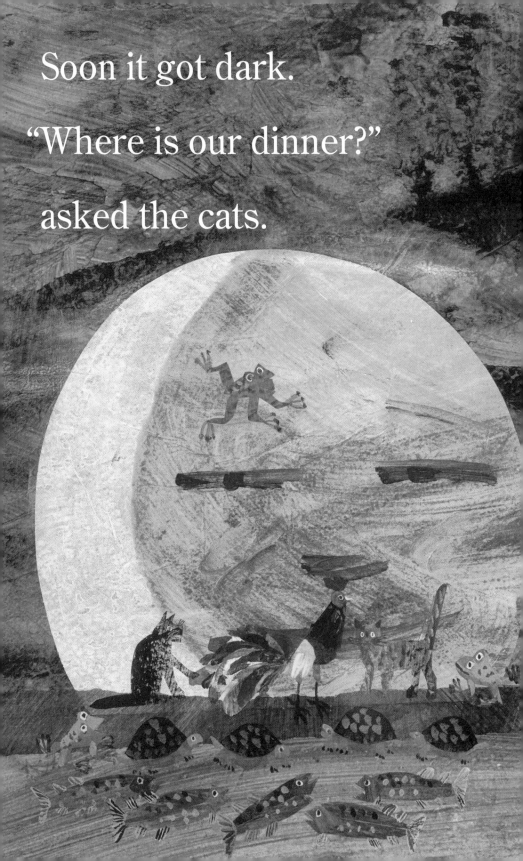

"Where do we sleep?"

asked the frogs.

"We are cold,"

said the turtles.

Fireflies flew up above.

"We are scared,"

said the fish.

The rooster did not

know what to say.

The fish wanted to go home,

so they swam away.

The turtles began to think

about their warm house.

They turned

and crawled back

down the road.

The frogs wanted

to go home too.

"Have a good evening,"

they said

as they jumped away

one by one.

The cats went home too.

"Have a good trip,"

they said.

Then the rooster

was all alone.

He had not seen the world.

The rooster looked
at the moon and said,
"I miss my home."

The moon did not answer.

It, too, went away.

The rooster turned
and went home.

He ate his grain and happily sat on his perch. Then he went to sleep.

The rooster had

a wonderful dream—

about a trip

around the world!